Divination and Disaster

MELISSA GUNN

ROSE KOWHAI PRODUCTIONS

Divination and Disaster

ISBN 978-1-0670066-9-3 ebook
ISBN 978-1-0670066-8-6 paperback print on demand

Contents

This book is written in New Zealand English. It may contain more 'u's and 's's than you're used to!

This one is for Mischief

Chapter One

THE TEST

I looked up from my test paper with a sense of impending doom. Sibylline tests—the ones which determine if you're able to be registered as a seer or not—are old-fashioned, paper-based exercises. I'd spent most of the last six years studying for the exam I'd just sat, and now it was over. I crossed all the fingers I could that I'd passed.

My whole family are seers. Every far-flung relative is engaged in some sort of clairvoyance or prophecy-based business. But I had a sinking feeling, as I watched the examiner read through my answers, that I would not be joining their ranks. That wasn't foreseeing; I just knew that I hadn't once experienced a seeing or vision. In particular, I had *seen* nothing during the past three hours of gruelling examination, despite having used scrying bowls, magic mirrors, runes, crystal balls, tarot cards, the works. The useless pieces of oracular equipment lay in accusing rows on the desks next to mine. I'd even tried listening to the wind in the leaves outside. That had just about sent me to sleep, but it hadn't told me anything other than that my late night up studying hadn't helped.

I'd written something for every question; my years of distance study had at least ensured that I knew which end of a pen was which, and advanced statistical modelling meant I could give a good guess. Of course, calculators weren't allowed in this exam, so I was mostly working with memories of probabilities. But guesses didn't count when you were supposed to prophecy.

The examiner, a middle-aged, black-haired woman in a grey cape and gown who I didn't know—she'd bussed in just for this test, and had only introduced herself as Ms Smith—beckoned for me to come up to the lectern which had been set up at one end of the classroom. I stood up, pushing back the uncomfortable school chair and surreptitiously shaking out my limbs as I walked over. I was well out of school, but the classroom had been the only place suitable for an exam in my rural hometown.

"This is the final test," she told me.

But the paper-based exam is the only thing they told me about. Panic gripped me by the throat.

"Tell me what my first name is," she said in a firm tone that brooked no nonsense.

Oh gods, this is like Rumpelstiltskin without the straw into gold part, I thought. *Focus, Sibyl.* I ran through the most common first names by year in my head. *She looked middle-aged. Let's say fifty years old. So... the most common girl's name in, say, 1970... That was a little out of the Susan period, Karen still made a good showing, but Michelle was moving up the ranks... of course, it depended on ethnicity too, but that could be so hard to judge...* I stared rudely at the woman for a moment. Her pale blue eyes stared back at me, but she didn't seem bothered by my scrutiny. *Maybe Irish?* Her accent didn't tell me anything. *Lisa, maybe? She's probably too old for Sarah.* I couldn't decide. I needed my modelling software to figure out a name, and even when using that there was a fair chance of getting it wrong.

"Fiona?" I asked at last, plumping for the Irish option.

"Is that your final answer?" she asked, making me doubt myself. I clutched my pencil so hard it broke.

"Er… Sharon? Um. No, Marama. Er…"

"Pick one, please. You may use a device if it helps you."

Her tone didn't give me any hints. I looked at the array of assistants to sight and knew that not one of them would help me.

"Rachel," I said, picking a name at random in desperation. "Your name is Rachel."

A smile blossomed on her face, crinkling the skin around her eyes. "Very close," she said. "My name is Rochelle. Now, take a seat while I mark your paper, and we'll see how you did."

Chapter Two

The examiner's eyes were unbearably kind as she looked up from my test paper.

"I'm sorry, dear," she said. 'But you haven't achieved a passing grade. I can't register you as a seer, and in fact I'd suggest you look into alternative job opportunities."

"I failed?" I asked, somehow needing to have it confirmed even though the woman had been perfectly clear. Standing up, I glared fiercely at the crystal ball ensconced in a velvet cloth in the middle of the desk full of *seeing* paraphernalia.

"Yes. You scored only 60 percent. Better than chance, but the sibylline guild has an 80 percent score in this test as a minimum entry requirement."

I stumbled back to my seat and sank into it, letting my head rest on my hands. "How could I fail?" I muttered, mostly to myself. "I've worked so hard."

The examiner walked over to me and rested her hands on my desk. I raised my head to look at her, resenting the invasion of my space all the more because I was fighting back tears.

"If you were meant to be a seer, you wouldn't have had to work hard," she said seriously.

The past few years of mind-bendingly hard work flashed through my mind. Wasted work. Wasted years. I'd put myself through endless remote courses and degrees, trying to catch up with my seer family by using probability and statistics with a large side helping of mythology. All for nothing.

I'd always known I was different from my family. Where they would automatically pack a bag with everything they'd need for the day, *knowing* what was coming, I would always have to guess.

A freak storm tearing its way through the river valley to the southeast of us? My Dad was on the phone to everyone we knew down that way with an evacuation plan before the storm even hit.

Surprise party? Never a thing for my sister, sometimes a thing for me (I got good at picking up little clues).

Friends dropping through on their way north or south? Mum started prepping before they'd left home, without them messaging first.

It was the only world I knew. Of *course* I tried to fit in. If only it wasn't so very hard.

Now, I'd been told it was impossible. The future yawned in front of me, an aching chasm of the unknown. That in itself was proof that my exam score wasn't a fluke.

I'd always been brought up to be polite, but it took all my will to mutter, "Thanks," to the examiner who'd brought my world crashing down around my ears before grabbing my bag and charging blindly out the door of the schoolroom. I only knocked one bag of runestones off the desks, and I didn't hear anything shatter, so it was probably all right.

Chapter Three

HOME TIME

I made my way home on foot. I could have biked, but I didn't want to get home any faster than necessary. The chances were also high that in my current state I'd ride my bike into the ditch, or turn the wheel on a stone I didn't see. Most of the roads aren't sealed round our way. I left my bike outside the school I'd long outgrown and trudged up the gravel road home. Usually on a hot day like this one, I'd scurry from one patch of shade to the next, but today it was all I could do to just put one foot after the other, wishing the cicada would stock their incessant trilling so I could think what on earth to do next.

"How did you go, love?" Mum asked when I came in, letting the back door close behind me with a bang. It was so unlike her to ask that I stopped dead, jolted out of my fug of misery.

"Don't you know?" I asked, letting the backpack with my failed paper in it slide off my shoulder to the floor.

"I purposely didn't *look*," she said. "Sometimes it's best not to know."

That told me she hadn't been sure I would pass. Not *seeing* was almost unheard-of for Mum.

"So?" She raised her dark eyebrows, clearly expecting an answer.

I opened my mouth to speak, and a sob tried to force its way out. I pressed my lips together, hard, and held out my hand with a thumb down, instead of speaking.

"Oh, Sibyl, I'm sorry." She closed the distance between us to engulf me in a much-needed hug, and I returned it, feeling the need for comfort. The sobs almost escaped again, but I kept them bottled up. I was in my twenties, after all, not a teenager—however much I felt like one, with the all-important exam failure crumbling my barriers.

"How about you take Rex for a walk," she suggested, releasing me. "He's been miserable, shut up inside while you were gone." She looked at me with a hint of a frown. "Do you want to choose dinner?"

"No thanks, Mum," I said. I could see she'd already started cooking; chopped herbs lay on a board on the bench, and sliced eggplant suggested some version of moussaka was on the menu. Dad usually cooked dessert. It made it hard for my sister and I to get a turn to cook, but we certainly ate well. Not that I felt like eating tonight.

I picked up my bag and headed down the hall to the room I'd lived in as long as I could remember, barring occasional trips to the beach an hour's drive away, or to some relative's farm. My dog, Rex, greeted me eagerly, jumping up to lick my face until I told him *no!* I'd had to leave him behind while I sat my exam. A shredded pillow told me he hadn't taken kindly to being left.

"Sorry, Rex. I had to do it alone," I told him. "But I failed. What do I do now?" The words came out in a wail, and I sank onto my bed and pulled my pillow over my head, overwhelmed by self-pity. The sobs that I'd held back earlier escaped now, and I silently howled my upset into the pillow, letting the soft fabric of the pillowcase absorb my tears.

Rex whined and crawled onto the bed beside me, which didn't leave much space. Rex was a German Shepherd. Not as big as some dogs, but big enough. His wet nose rootled under the pillow until he could snuffle in my ear. I laughed through my tears and sat up to give him a hug. He thumped his tail against the bed, then pulled away to jump down and stand by the door.

"You're right, I need to give you a walk," I agreed after a bit. Anything was better than the black hole of misery I could feel myself spiralling into.

Chapter Four

THE FAMILY REACTS

The walk—around the edge of the paddocks up to the wind turbine, then back around the long way—cleared my head a little. I stood under the wind turbine for as long as Rex would let me, gazing out over the forested hills. An old trading trail wound along the ridgeline, and I imagined following it, meeting people along the way. An unfamiliar tug of longing pulled at me. What if I did go? Not just along the ridge, but out into the wide world? Seers tended to live away from big cities, and my family was no exception.

Our tiny rural town was barely a dot on the map. What would it be like to live in a city, where every neighbour didn't know your name? Where you could reinvent yourself with ease?

Then I shook my head. What could I do away from the place I'd lived my whole life? And besides, the times I'd toyed with the idea of moving out, I'd seen that pet-friendly rentals were like gold nuggets: often dreamed of, rarely found, even when you looked really hard. I couldn't move to a city without Rex, and another small town didn't appeal. I couldn't see a way to explore that future. Then I snorted in self-disgust. I'd just failed my seeing exams, of course I couldn't *see* a way forward. I gave Rex a click of my tongue and started downhill again. Rex ranged around me, running after rabbit trails then circling back to check on me, tongue lolling in the heat, tail waving high in the air.

When Delphine met me outside the house and said 'bad luck,' before I could say anything, I had pulled myself together enough that I could nod in acknowledgement without bursting into tears.

"You can still help like you always do," she suggested, falling into step beside me and Rex as we walked up the garden path.

Dad was the gardener of the family in his off hours, and he'd created a Greek-inspired rockery garden out the front of our white-painted weatherboard house. The kumara beds were around the back, sheltered from the frosts by a hedge of feijoas which dropped perfumed green fruits all over the lawn every autumn. Lavender, thyme and rosemary all but swamped the actual rocks of the rockery. The lavender and thyme were in full bloom but I gazed past them unseeing today.

"I'm not sure," I told Delphine.

Five years my junior, Delphine was full of excitement at the prospect of a career as a seer. She would no doubt pass her sibylline exam with flying colours. She had just finished school, but had no interest in pursuing online degrees as I had.

"I can see for you if you like," she offered.

"*No!*" My refusal came out more emphatically than I meant it to and she recoiled.

"I only offered," she said. "No need to bite my head off." She stalked ahead of me, and *didn't* leave the door open.

I released Rex into the garden after giving him a bowl of water and a good hug and a scratch behind the ears, then entered the house, knowing I'd have to face my whole family sooner or later.

It turned out it was sooner. Delphine, Mum, and Dad were all in the sitting room with the TV on ready for the news at six. Delphine glared, but Mum stood up and gave me a hug.

"I'm sorry, Sibyl," she said. She sounded like she meant it.

Dad muted the TV and stood too. He's not much of a hugger, but he gave me a side-shoulder squeeze.

"Your cousin Tim has a new cabin on that farm of his. Why don't you and Rex take a week off?" he suggested.

I seized on the opportunity for distraction greater than remaining in my tiny hometown.

"That could be good," I said cautiously.

"But that new set of predictions has just come in for checking," Delphine objected. "It's a huge job. We need the help even if Sibyl *can't* see."

"Delphine." Dad's voice was stern. "We'll handle it."

"Take a break, love," Mum encouraged me. "A week or so away will give you some time to regroup." She released me from the hug and turned away to pour everyone a pre-dinner glass of iced water. It was a hot day, and the ice was already half melted in the glasses she must have brought through earlier.

Dad unmuted the TV and sat down again, ready to hear what the markets were doing, as though he hadn't spent much of the day listening to the leaves of the trees to see what they had to tell him about global finances. Mum was more of a scrying-bowl type of seer, and Delphine currently favoured crystal balls—though that could change as soon as a new fad in seeing-ware came through.

I couldn't imagine that a week would make any difference to my outlook when I'd just failed the most important exam of my life, but I was prepared to go to Tim's farm just for a change of scene. I definitely needed time to reassess my life choices.

Chapter Five

My cousin came to pick me up the next day. He was a few years older than me, though not so much older that he didn't remember sitting his own seers exam.

"Hard luck, Sib," he said. "But a bit of hard work on the farm will see you right."

I couldn't agree with him in good conscience, so I said nothing.

Tim closed the door to his ute and dropped to one knee in front of Rex, who'd accompanied me out the front door.

"Who's the best boy, eh?" He spoke directly to Rex, and ruffled the fur behind Rex's ears in a way that would usually make Rex back away growling. Oddly enough, Rex stood there and took it, even condescending to wag his tail a little. He caught me looking at him and whined.

"Good boy, Rex," I told him. I couldn't help sounding a little dull and tired. I hadn't slept last night, staring into the familiar darkness of my bedroom and wondering what to do with myself now.

Tim finished patting my dog and reached for my backpack. "That all you got?" he asked as he slung it onto the back of the ute.

"That's all," I said numbly. Everything was numb today. Even my behind, from three hours of sitting in a hard school chair yesterday.

"Righto. Up you get, Rex," he said, patting the back of the ute so Rex knew where to go.

There was no-one to see me off. The rest of the family was busy at work in the various offices that masqueraded as farm sheds and garages. Solar panel arrays and satellite dishes decorated their roofs so the family could keep connected with the markets. I hadn't wanted to fail my exam, but I couldn't be sad *not* to be inside on a hot summer's day. Tim didn't say much as we roared down the road, raising dust which coated the shrubs on the road verges. The vehicle was loud enough that it would be awkward to talk even if I'd felt like it. Instead, I rolled down my window and let the hot wind wash over my face.

Tim's farm was on an unmarked gravel road off the Thermal Explorer highway, and while he'd been one of the first people Dad called when he got wind of the big storm, there hadn't been a lot he could do to avoid the effects of the landslides the storm had caused. I hadn't seen the farm since that storm, and the size of the scars on the landscape shocked me out of my numbness.

"No wonder you wanted a hand," I exclaimed, sitting up straighter to look around as Tim swung off the road and onto a potholed driveway.

Tim nodded—although it could have just been the jolting of the potholes.

"Yeah, she was a big one," he agreed. "One of those times I wished I'd got a dog to keep me company, too." He looked at Rex in the rear-view mirror. My dog was balancing expertly on the flatbed of the ute, looking eagerly around. "Reckon there's any more out there like your Rex?"

"Probably not." I didn't feel like extolling Rex's virtues.

"Ah well, let's get you sorted." He pulled up in front of a tiny one-room cabin and killed the engine. "This is the first of my ecotourism chalets. Flash, right?"

"Sure, Tim," I agreed automatically.

Tim's seer business is in animal feed predictions, but he's always after an easier, faster way to make money. For the first time it occurred to me to wonder if Tim was actually very good at *seeing*. Had he passed his sibylline exams? He must have done, but perhaps he didn't actually like to prophecy. Maybe that's why Dad was always giving him oracular advice. Or maybe he just felt the need since Tim's mum and dad had moved overseas a few years back, and weren't on hand for the sort of hand-holding that Dad liked to provide.

I brushed road dust off myself as I got out of the vehicle and looked over the cabin. It looked like one of the sheds that housed my family's business, but without the solar panels or satellite dishes. The cabin had a corrugated iron roof, plywood sides, and an absence of anything growing for about a metre all around it. It looked out over a sloping paddock which held a pond at the bottom. In the right light, it could be great. Right now the harsh sun was directly overhead. There was no shade anywhere, and pink and green pondweed made a thick surface on top of the pond. It was definitely *not* the right light.

"Tourists like flowers, don't they?" I asked as I looked at the desolate expanse around the cabin.

"Do they?" Tim said disingenuously. "I guess that can be your first job then. Bung a few plants in the ground. Your Dad left some last time he was here, they're round the back of the main house."

Sounded like a typical seer action. My family regularly demonstrated their foresight, the ability I lacked. All. The. Time.

I gritted my teeth, holding back a curse (which knowing my luck, would actually be effective. While I wasn't able to see to save myself, the few charms and wards required in a small town like ours had never given me any trouble).

"Sure, Tim. I'll get right on that. And sort out a water feature for your pond, too. Having a water feature gives a statistically higher chance of having high occupancy rates in tourist rentals." I'd come across the statistic somewhere, but this was the first time it had been useful. Still, information's like that—you never know when you're going to need it. I clenched my fists, remembering yesterday's exam. All that information hadn't helped me then. But that wasn't Tim's fault.

"Awesome!"

"Although they could have meant spa pools. It was an assignment for the degree before my last one."

"You ever going to do anything with those degrees?" Tim asked.

Was that wistfulness in his voice? Tim hadn't done any tertiary education, but I didn't think he'd felt the need for it either. He'd bought this farm straight out of school after a lucky break with a hay stockpile and a grass shortage. Of course, he'd claimed he'd seen it. Maybe he had.

"As soon as you've let me unpack, I'll plant your flowers in a scholarly way. Is there somewhere for Rex?" Rex, who'd been sniffing around the base of the cabin, bounded over when I said his name. I gave him a quick pat to reward his attentiveness.

Tim rubbed the back of his head. "Well, you know I didn't get another dog after Beaut passed away, right?"

I nodded my understanding. That had been a few years ago. Tim had fostered a couple of dogs since, but not kept one, claiming none lived up to his previous dog.

"Yeah, well, the thing is, I thought her old kennel would be more use in a rescue place, so I donated it."

I sighed and gave Tim a pat on the shoulder, the same way I'd patted Rex. "That was kind of you," I said. I thought I understood the unspoken emotion behind that decision. "I'll just have Rex in with me. If you don't mind your tourist cabin getting sprinkled with dog hair."

Tim grinned, his relief clear. It was a good thing Rex was more of a pet than a working dog, but I'd no doubt have to bathe him before letting him into my cabin.

"Nah, she'll be right. I'll just advertise it as pet-friendly and charge twice as much."

He stepped up onto the tiny deck that made a step into the cabin and opened the door. "There y'go. Beauty, isn't she?"

I levered off my shoes and stepped into the cabin, expecting more of Tim's rustic approach to ecotourism inside.

"Wow!" I was truly amazed. While Tim hadn't grasped the basics of attractive landscaping (or perhaps just hadn't yet had time—the deck looked brand new), the interior of the cabin lived up to his hype. Polished timber floors gleamed in sunlight which flooded in from a skylight. A four-poster bed with gauzy curtains filled the far end of the cabin and attractive wallpaper covered the walls. A wooden counter flanked the entrance, with a bar fridge and an oven tucked under the gleaming wood. A kettle and a basket of assorted tea bags sat next to a coffee plunger and a bowl of feijoas. A comfortable-looking chair was angled so that anyone sitting in it could see either the large flatscreen TV, or the view out of the cabin's large window. "Did you get someone to design this?" I asked, my astonishment making my voice rise questioningly.

"Nah, Delphine sent over a link to a bed-and-breakfast website, so I sat down and had a good look at what was going to be popular, then ordered that. Feed predictions are my bread and butter, but it's nice to have a bit extra going on." He looked pleased at my approval. I never understood Tim very well, even when he'd been my closest cousin, living just down the road, but there was no doubt he'd done well with this cabin.

"It looks great." I put all the enthusiasm I could muster into my voice, and he grinned.

"Glad you like it. You can leave the first review. I'll let you dump your stuff. Just head over to the main house when you're ready to get planting and I'll give you the tools. Aunt Pythia said there'll be enough rain to get them watered in, so that's all good."

"And are you helping me with this effort?" I asked suspiciously.

"Yeah, nah. I've got a bunch of predictions to make for the autumn harvest season. I'll give you a hand if you're not done by the time I finish those. And tomorrow, there are some fences to replace."

I groaned. I'd forgotten how much hard work there was to do on a farm. Still, the point was to get away from my daily routine, and there was no doubt I'd done that.

Chapter Six

I found the plants before I found Tim. They were arranged in rows in a shadehouse behind the main house, which was further up the driveway, sheltered by a stand of mature trees whose roots had obviously been deep enough to revive the storm that caused the landslides.

I'd expected perhaps a few punnets of bedding plants, perhaps some small shrubs. Knowing Dad had left the plants, I thought there would almost certainly be some feijoas. He told us once, proudly, that he'd planted a feijoa at every house he'd lived in, anywhere. I did find several feijoas, but there must have been over a hundred plants in that shadehouse, ranging from native flaxes and shrubs to the bedding plants that I'd expected. There was even a small lemon tree, and a bucket held some unpromising lumps labelled as waterlilies.

I stormed up to Tim's back door (since it was closer to the shadehouse than the front door) and thumped on it. Rex jumped excitedly when Tim opened the door, an ear of dried corn in his hand and his dark hair spiked up in random directions.

"Just how many hands do you think I have?" I demanded. "There's a week's worth of planting in that shadehouse."

Tim's puzzled expression cleared. "Yeah. Auntie Helen dropped off some plants too. Said you'd need to be kept busy."

I frowned, my anger diverted. "When was that?"

Counting on his fingers, Tim looked up at the ceiling. "About three days ago," he said, looking back at me. "Problem?"

My anger returned in full force. "Yes, problem. *I* didn't know I was going to fail three days ago." Tears welled up before I could stop them, my anger mixing with upset. "Why did any of them even let me sit the stupid exam if they knew I was going to fail?"

Tim shuffled his feet and said nothing.

Blinking the tears away, I glared at him. "Did you know?"

"No, no," he said hastily, taking a step back into his dimly lit house. "I only predict animal feed futures, you know that." He waved the corn in front of him defensively. "Look, I'll help with the planting as soon as I'm done, alright?" He looked at Rex. "Rex can sit with me if he's bored," he added, almost hopefully.

"Right," I muttered. I didn't have the heart to argue with Tim any more. Buying this farm had been his one big break, and he'd never been one to interfere. Probably just got bossed around by my mum, my dad, our mutual aunts, and probably everyone else, too. "I look forward to your help," I said at last.

"Er, yeah. Great." Tim directed another glance inside, where he no doubt had some sort of complicated stock-feed-prediction foretelling on the go. "I'll just get on with it then." Patting Rex on the head, he closed the door, leaving me standing looking at the pale, sun-blistered wood.

Chapter Seven

THE RAIN ARRIVES

It took three days for Tim to finish his predictions. After that, it took both of us two more days to finish the planting. Rex hung around and chased sticks whenever Tim flung them. He really seemed to like my cousin a lot. The first lot of plants were looking dry and wilted by the end of that time. Fortunately, on the evening of the fifth day, the rain set in.

After the first hour of torrential downpour and boredom (I hadn't brought enough books along for this length of stay, and with no satellite dish for internet access, I couldn't get more), I looked out the window and realised that the driveway had turned into a stream. The water feature I'd said was lacking when I first arrived was now present, and cascading down the hill. I donned a raincoat and went to find Tim. Rex accompanied me, apparently happy to trot through the rain.

"You are *not* going to lie on my bed after this," I told him, watching the rain peppering his hairy flanks. He wagged his tail.

Tim wasn't in the house. I went so far as to enter the building and check every room. The front room, facing the road, was obviously his seer centre of operations, because there were bowls of dry corn kernels, several types of pellets in different sizes, a few types of grain, and a hank of hay, arranged on a big table with something like a ouija board in the middle of it. *So that's what animal feed predicting looks like.* Part of me wanted to laugh, but the rest of me was just sad, because Tim had an ability to turn the ridiculous-looking assortment into predictions. And apparently that was something I'd never be capable of.

Leaving the house, I checked the shadehouse, which was now empty of everything including Tim. I paused under the large macrocarpa as the downpour, improbably, intensified. The piney scent of the tree was strong in the rain, overpowering the smell of mud and ozone. I inhaled it gratefully.

If this was the prophesied rain, it was on the heavy side for plant watering. Not to mention it was summer, so such heavy rain was out of season. Thunder grumbled in the distance and Rex pressed against my leg, his tail losing its enthusiastic wag. I couldn't hear him whimper, but I could feel his body vibrating with fear. He'd never been a fan of electrical storms. I glanced up at the tree above me. Perhaps I should move.

Shelter was nice, but being electrocuted was not something I wanted to try out.

"Come on Rex, we'll go back to the house and wait for Tim there."

We dashed through the rain toward the main house, which was a lot closer than my fancy cabin. We were only halfway there when lightning crackled through the sky, so close I could hear it sizzle. I flung myself forward, and reached the shelter of the back porch just as thunder boomed, shaking both me and the house. I looked around for Rex. He had made it to the house before I did, and was scrabbling at the door handle with his front paws. That was a new trick. As I watched, dripping torrents of water onto the wooden floor of the porch, Rex got the door open, then trotted inside, turning his head to look back at me. His tongue lolled out in a doggy laugh. Now he was out of the storm, he was completely at ease.

"Well done then, you goofy dog," I told him.

He shook himself off, showering everything with mud and water.

"Ugh, don't do that again!"

I was at a loss now. It wasn't safe to go back outside, but where was Tim? Taking off my raincoat, I hung it beside the row of blue overalls that Tim kept for working on the farm, and left it to drip dry. The temperature had dropped with the storm, so I went into the kitchen and put the kettle on. If Tim was out in this weather, he'd probably want something hot when he returned.

Chapter Eight

MISSING IN ACTION

As the sky grew darker and the storm showed no sign of abating, I grew more worried.

"What's he doing, Rex?" I asked my dog, in the absence of anyone else to ask. I checked my emails for the hundredth time, not because I thought anything important would arrive—there was still no internet, after all—but for something to do. As I did so, a notification flashed for a text message. It was from my sister, Delphine.

Send Rex to find Tim, the message read. There was another notification a second later. *Do it now.*

Honestly, life with seers was crazy. But if it was so important that Delphine sent a second message, I had better do as she said.

"All right, Delphine," I muttered. Then I called Rex, who had been lying on the rug in front of the unlit fire, looking rather more mournful than he usually did. Perhaps the kibble I'd brought along didn't agree with him. Or perhaps it was just the continuing storm.

"Rex, find Tim?"

Rex lifted his head immediately, ears pricked. Apparently this was what he'd been waiting for. "Do you think you can find Tim, Rex?"

He scrambled to his feet and bounded to the front door, where he performed the same trick as he had done with the back door. Before I could haul on my raincoat, he was off and out the door.

"Wait for me, Rex!"

Unusually, he ignored me and charged off into the night. Giving up the struggle with my damp raincoat, I settled for putting the hood on and treating the rest of it like a cloak. At least it kept off some of the rain as I set off down the driveway after Rex. At least, I hoped I was following Rex. It was too dark to see him now, and unlike the brightly lit cities I'd dreamed of visiting, the country night wasn't alleviated by streetlights. I couldn't even see lights from the nearest neighbours, a few kilometres in either direction.

Wind whipped at my raincoat, driving the rain inside it. I clutched it closed with one hand and focussed on keeping my balance. It was like walking in a stream.

"Rex? Tim?" I called as I walked, every few minutes. I passed the cabin, my eyes adjusted to the darkness enough now that I could see it as a darker lump against the dark sky. At least the lightning seemed to have moved on for now. I called again, and thought I heard a bark downhill.

I kept going until I was nearly at the end of the driveway. The pond that I usually viewed from my cabin had overflowed its banks and was lapping halfway across the drive. I stopped there. Should I keep going? Would I be cut off from the farm if I did? And how did I even know this was the way Rex had come? I called one more time. And this time, there was an answer. Not a bark, but a shout.

"Sib! This way, Sib!"

The shout came from the direction of the pond. I felt around until I found the fence, and moved along that—hoping it wasn't electrified—until I came to a gate. An open gate, the number one, cardinal offence on a farm. Either Tim had been working on the fences here or someone else had come in and left the gate open. A chill of unease prickled the hair on the back of my neck—or possibly that was a stray raindrop. Either way, Tim's call meant he needed my help. I splashed through the open gate, cursing as the water topped my gumboots and immediately made walking more of a waddle than a stride. I kept going, skirting what I hoped were the shallower edges of the pond. You never knew what might be living in a pond like that one. It was unlikely to hold a bunyip—we don't get many of those in this country, they prefer their native Australia—but all kinds of water dwellers had come along with European colonists, from grindylow to rusalka, and there was always the chance of a taniwha.

"Tim?" I called once again.

"Over here." A familiar bark followed Tim's words.

I'd reached the far side of the pond, where rushes and raupō met kanuka scrub. It was even darker under the trees, but movement caught my eye. Tim was waving to catch my attention. He leaned up against a tree trunk, and one arm wrapped firmly around Rex.

"Oh, man, Sib, am I glad to see you and Rex!" Tim gave Rex a squeeze, and rather than protesting with a growl the way he usually would, Rex turned and gave Tim's face a lick. "Give me a hand up will you?" Tim said.

I hurried forward and offered a hand. Tim was bigger and bulkier than me, and he almost pulled me over when I tried to haul him up, but somehow neither of us toppled.

"What happened? Are you all right?" I asked, giving Rex a pat myself. "Good boy," I added.

Tim reached out and leaned on my shoulder before hopping forward into the splash zone. I took a step to stay with him, then another. It looked like it would be a long slog up the hill.

"I was working on the fence down here," he said. "When the storm began, I thought I'd wait it out under the trees. But then things started turning weird. Some bikes went past, but I heard one turn up the drive. Probably turned back when they saw the dog warning signs, I reckon." He grinned at me, white teeth flashing in the dark. "Good job we did those ones, eh?" We'd installed those signs in breaks between planting sessions, a day ago. Digging the holes with a post hole borer had just about done me in. The longer I worked here with Tim, the more sure I was that farm work wasn't the long-term career I wanted.

"Glad they did something," I agreed.

"Yeah. Anyway, after that, the lightning began. One strike just about hit the pond, I thought I was a goner for sure. But when I could see again, there was some serious rustling in the bushes behind me. I'd just about made up my mind to run for home when this whopping great pig pops out of the pond and charges at me. I fair ran for it, but it got me in the leg. I thought I was a goner again. But then Rex here popped out of the dark and came in like a wild thing and chased it off. So I sat tight and waited for you to turn up too. And here we are." Tim paused long enough to pat Rex again, then resumed his slow hop.

I didn't know what to say. I wanted to start with 'lucky Delphine texted', but I knew it wasn't luck.

"You didn't see any of that in advance?" I asked.

"Just the bit about Rex," he said, surprisingly cheerful for someone who'd been gored by a boar. "I don't usually see stuff outside of animal feed. But I booked a doctor in for tomorrow, so I just need you to get me to the house. He'll be coming by in the morning."

Trust Tim to know a doctor who still did house visits.

"No wonder you were so glad to see Rex," I said. I still couldn't understand why Rex was so nice to Tim though. "Um, do you think that pig is still around somewhere?" There were a lot of pigs in the hills (maybe we needed more werewolves), but I'd hate to meet one in the dark, with an injured man. And I much though I loved Rex, one dog was not usually enough to keep an angry pig at bay. I'd heard stories of what they could do.

"I reckon the lightning scared it," he said. "That's why it moved so fast."

That wasn't really an answer, but I was having enough of a hard time sloshing through the water, taking as much as I could of Tim's weight, and trying to make sure we didn't end up *in* the pond with all the water coming down the hill.

Chapter Nine

An age later we made it to the driveway again. I tipped water and pondweed out of my gumboots. Tim sat down and did the same. Then I had to help heave him up again. Rex stalked around us while we did so. He seemed on edge, and I couldn't blame him.

"Do you think I should go get the ute?" I asked Tim. It would be easier than walking all the way back up the driveway again.

But Tim looked at the way Rex was walking, stiff-legged and wary.

"Nah, better to stay together," he said.

So we limped up the hill. It was the hardest thing I'd done in my life, even worse than five days of planting, or studying calculus, or sitting that awful sibylline exam. My whole side ached from supporting Tim, and the rain kept coming down, and I would have been frozen with cold except that I was hot from the effort. Rex stalked behind us the whole way back. But we made it to my cabin at last.

"This is far enough," I said firmly. Tim didn't argue. As I opened the door, Rex barked once. He dashed up to me, leaped high enough to lick my face, then dashed off back down the hill. "Rex!" I shouted. "Come back!" But he didn't come.

Tim made it inside and collapsed onto the chair. "I'll wait here for the doc," he said.

I hesitated by the door, wanting to shut out the storm and any wild pigs, but wanting to leave Rex a way in. Improbably, my phone pinged again. I must only have reception at the top of the hill. I stepped inside and pulled out the phone, wiping some of the moisture off it. It was another message from Delphine.

Don't wait for Rex. He'll be back, but not while you're at the farm.

The chill that coursed through me this time was definitely from more than just the cold. What did she mean? Gods, life with seers was just too much. No matter what happened, someone saw the outcome and told me about it. It was enough to drive anyone mad.

I reluctantly closed the door. I guessed I should see if Tim needed any first aid, now we were somewhere that I could offer it. Tim had equipped the cabin with a first aid kit, which I'd found days ago when I needed something to treat my digging-induced blisters. I quickly located it again and approached with alcohol wipes and bandages. Tim opened his eyes for a moment.

"You'll need to keep me stable overnight, but the doc will arrive in time to take over. Call your Mum, she'll be able to pick you up and take you home. Oh, and my neighbour Sheryl will pop by later tomorrow and stay for a few days, leading to an interesting relationship which I'll pursue once I'm up and about again. Also, don't wait for Rex, he won't return until after you've moved on. Plus the boar was a supernatural animal sent by Artemis to signal that a change is required."

I blinked at him, wanting to take him up on Rex, but also blindsided by his sudden loquacity. "I thought you just did animal feed predictions."

"Broadly, yes. With some exceptions for my personal wellbeing." Tim closed his eyes again. "I'm done in. Just bandage up my leg, then I'll sleep on the bed and you can have the chair. OK?"

I bit my lip to hold in my curses. "Sure. That'll work out *just fine.*" I don't think Tim heard my words, because he began to snore. Maybe I'd get the bed after all. Not that I was likely to sleep with Rex out in a storm, and the info-dump of divination that Tim had spouted. I ripped open the alcohol wipes and prepared to inflict as much cleaning on Tim's gored wound as I could. This farm visit had turned into a disaster.

Sometime in the night Tim lurched upright and staggered over to the bed, which I'd retreated to after doing my best with the wound on his calf. Grumbling, I dragged a pillow and extra blanket over to the chair and settled there. Tim's snores made sure I didn't get any sleep. During the long dark hours, my brain had whirred and buzzed through dozens of different plans and strategies for a new life. Whatever I did, I decided, I had to get away from all my seer relatives. Living amongst seers when I clearly wasn't one made me feel like I was missing something vital, like missing a hand or a foot. I wanted to feel whole.

The next morning turned out exactly as Tim had predicted. I was reluctant to climb into Mum's car when she turned up, wheels sliding on the driveway where the night's rain had washed gravel off the clay.

"You're sure you'll be all right here till Sheryl turns up?" Mum asked Tim.

Gods, she hadn't even asked about his prediction. She must have done her own bit of seeing.

"Yep, just drop me off at my house before you go. I've got some ration packs over there," Tim replied. "Thanks for the rescue, Sib, you were a star."

My heart warmed a little at the praise. It's always nice to have your efforts appreciated, after all.

Tim limped to the passenger seat, and Mum and I helped lower him in for the short drive to the main house. We deposited him on a sofa in his lounge, with a meal and a drink at hand on a small table.

"Good job on the planting, too," Tim said as we turned to go.

Mum drove me slowly past the cabin, casting a critical eye over the place.

"He's going to do well out of this one," she decreed.

I looked over my work of the last few days. The rain was still misting in, raindrops rolling off long flax leaves and forming drips on smaller plants. The storm had carved a watercourse through the paddock, and a small waterfall sprayed prettily into the pond, which looked empty of anything but water and pondweed by daylight. Or, no, not quite empty. A water lily had opened up in the centre of the muddy water, pink and yellow petals glowing in a sudden sunbeam that made its way through the low cloud.

I could see, even without the gift of divination, that the cabin would look great once the plants had grown a bit. I rolled my aching shoulders. They were a reminder that while it was a good feeling to create something that looked nice, farm work and landscaping didn't feel like my fortune. No, whatever my future might hold, I wanted to take a different route. Something unforeseen. It would take planning to escape my seer family, but the time had definitely come.

THE END

Also by Melissa Gunn

Weather Gods series:

Flash Flood

Storm Surge

Heat Wave

Woodside Cosy Urban Fantasy Series:

Seers and Salt

Short stories & novellas:

Treescape (First published in Magic and Mystery: A limited Edition Urban Fantasy Mystery Anthology)
Feels Like Heaven (in Aftermath: Stories of Survival in Aotearoa New Zealand)
First Pav on Mars (in Pav Deconstructed, Pavlova Press)
A Gift of Coconuts (Imagine 2200 2024 collection)